ISBN: 9798357491190

www.samirataj.com

This Book Belongs To:

_____

Santa

Christmas Crossword

"Christmas day"

join the dots - trace the lines - color in

5

FIND TWO
THE SAME
PICTURES
?

FIND TWO
THE SAME
PICTURES
?

6

color by number

| 1 | 2 | 3 | 4 | 5 | 6 | 7 | 8 |

dark blue   blue   dark green   green   yellow   brown   orange   black

finish the alphabet - color in

8

9

color me in

Santa- copy and color

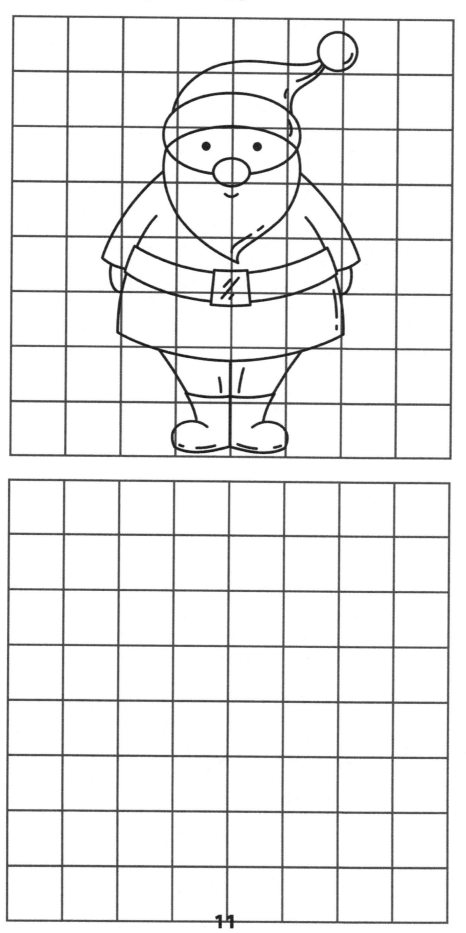

find 7 differences then color in

join dots - trace lines - color in

how many?

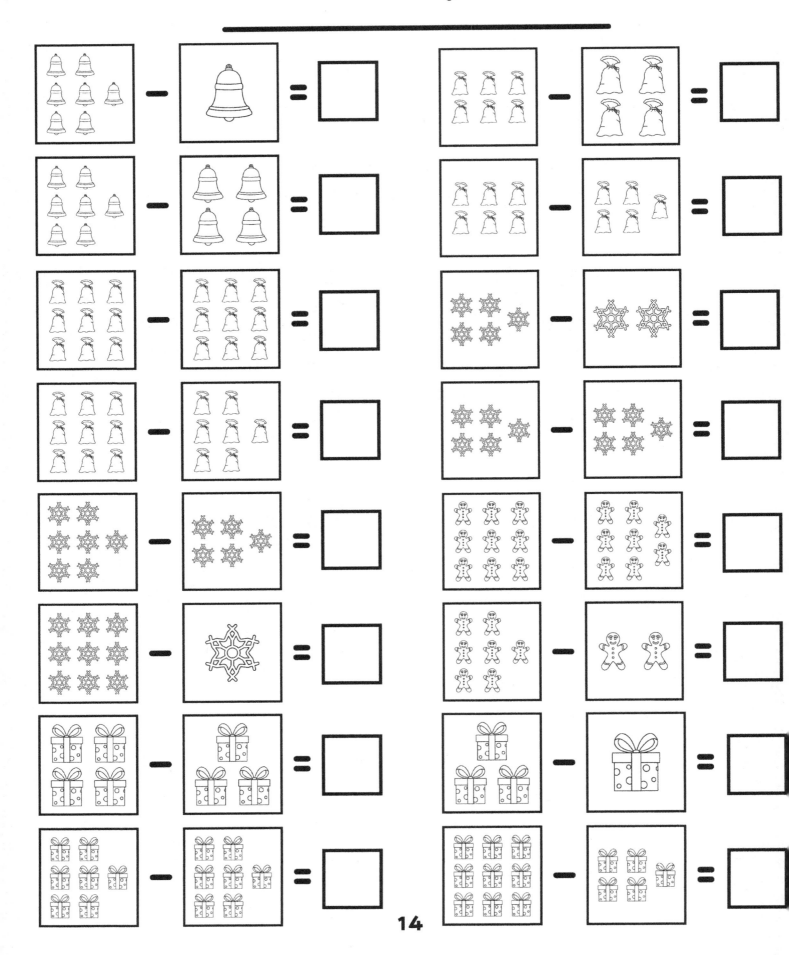

color by numbers

1	1	1	1	1	1	1	1	1	1	1	1	1	1	1	1	1	1	1	1	1	1	1	1	1	1	1	1	1	1
1	1	1	1	1	1	1	1	1	1	4	4	4	4	4	1	1	1	1	1	1	1	1	1	1	1	1	1	1	1
1	1	1	1	1	1	1	1	1	4	4	4	3	4	4	2	2	1	1	1	1	1	1	1	1	1	1	1	1	1
1	1	1	1	1	1	1	1	4	4	4	4	4	1	1	2	2	1	1	1	1	1	1	1	1	1	1	1	1	1
1	1	1	1	1	1	1	4	4	4	4	4	4	1	1	1	1	1	1	1	1	1	1	1	1	1	1	1	1	1
1	1	1	1	1	1	3	3	3	3	3	3	3	3	3	1	1	1	1	1	1	1	1	1	1	1	1	1	1	1
1	1	1	1	1	1	3	2	2	2	2	2	2	2	3	1	1	1	1	1	1	1	1	1	1	1	1	1	1	1
1	1	1	1	1	2	2	2	2	2	2	2	2	2	2	2	1	1	1	1	1	1	1	1	1	1	1	1	1	1
1	1	1	1	1	2	2				5				2	2	1	1	1	1	1	1	1	1	1	1	1	1	1	1
1	1	3	3	1	2		5	6	5	5	5	6	5		2	1	1	1	1	1	1	1	1	1	1	1	1	1	1
1	1	3	3	1	1	5	5	5	5	5	5	5	5	5	1	1	1	1	1	1	1	1	1	1	1	1	1	1	1
1	1	3	3	3	3		5	5				5	5		1	1	1	1	1	1	1	1	1	1	1	1	1	1	1
1	1	3	3	3	1		5		5		5			1	1	1	1	1	1	1	1	1	1	1	1	1	1	1	1
1	2	2	2	2	1	1						1	1	1	1	1	1	1	1	1	1	1	1	1	1	1	1	1	1
1	1	4	4	3	1	4	3				3	4	1	1	1	1	1	1	1	1	1	1	1	1	1	1	1	1	1
1	1	4	4	4	4	4	4	3		3	4	4	1	1	1	1	1	1	1	1	1	1	1	1	1	1	1	1	1
1	1	4	4	4	4	3	4	3	2	3	4	4	4	4	1	1	1	1	1	1	1	1	1	1	1	1	1	1	1
1	1	1	4	4	3	3	4	4	4	2	4	4	4	4	4	1	1	1	1	1	1	1	1	1	1	1	1	1	1
1	1	1	1	1	1	3	4	4	7	7	7	4	4	3	4	4	4	1	1	1	1	1	1	1	1	1	1	1	1
1	1	1	1	1	1	6	6	6	7	6	7	6	6	6	3	4	4	8	1	1	1	1	1	1	1	1	1	1	1
1	1	1	1	1	4	4	4	4	7	7	7	4	4	4	3	3	2	2	8	7	1	1	1	1	1	1	1	1	1
1	1	1	1	1	4	4	4	4	4	2	4	4	4	4	4	2	3	3	8	7	1	1	1	1	1	1	1	1	1
1	1	1	1	1	1	4	4	4	4	2	4	4	4	4	4	3	3	3	1	1	1	1	1	1	1	1	1	1	1
1	1	1	1	1	2	2	2	2	2	2	2	2	2	2	2	1	3	3	1	1	1	1	1	1	1	1	1	1	1
1	1	1	1	1	1	1	3	3	3	1	3	3	3	1	1	1	7	8	1	1	1	1	1	1	1	1	1	1	1
1	1	1	1	1	1	4	4	4	1	4	4	4	1	1	8	7	7	7	8	1	1	1	1	1	1	1	1	1	1
1	1	1	1	1	1	4	4	4	1	4	4	4	1	7	7	8	8	8	8	1	1	1	1	1	1	1	1	1	1
1	1	1	1	1	1	6	6	6	1	6	6	6	1	8	7	8	7	7	7	8	1	1	1	1	1	1	1	1	1
1	1	1	1	1	1	6	6	6	1	6	6	6	7	7	7	8	7	8	7	8	1	1	1	1	1	1	1	1	1
1	1	1	1	1	1	6	6	6	1	6	6	6	8	8	8	8	7	7	7	8	1	1	1	1	1	1	1	1	1
1	1	1	1	1	1	6	6	6	6	1	6	6	6	6	7	7	8	8	8	8	8	1	1	1	1	1	1	1	1
1	1	1	1	1	1	1	1	1	1	1	1	1	1	1	1	1	1	1	1	1	1	1	1	1	1	1	1	1	1
1	1	1	1	1	1	1	1	1	1	1	1	1	1	1	1	1	1	1	1	1	1	1	1	1	1	1	1	1	1

1 - light green   2 - light blue   3 - dark red   4 - red

5 - beige   6 - black   7 - yellow   8 - blue

trace the lines

christmas word search

STOCKING

SANTA

SNOWMAN

SNOWGLOBE

DEER

PRESENT

S	N	O	W	M	A	N
C	S	T	O	P	R	S
S	N	O	C	H	E	A
D	E	W	K	R	S	N
S	E	G	I	I	E	T
T	R	L	N	G	N	A
M	A	O	B	E	T	S

trace the alphabet

Aa Bb Cc Dd
Ee Ff Gg Hh
Ii Jj Kk Ll
Mm Nn Oo Pp
Qq Rr Ss Tt
Uu Vv Ww Xx
Yy Zz

MATCH THE SAME QUANTITY

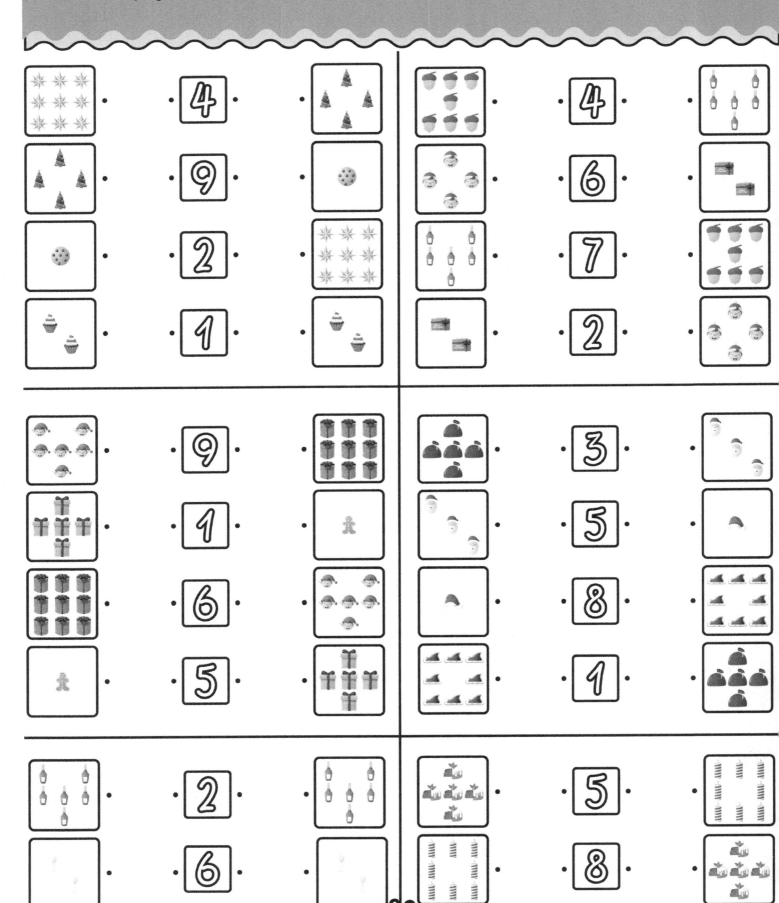

doto to dot - trace lines - color in

find 10 differences then color in

who gets to the present?

color by code

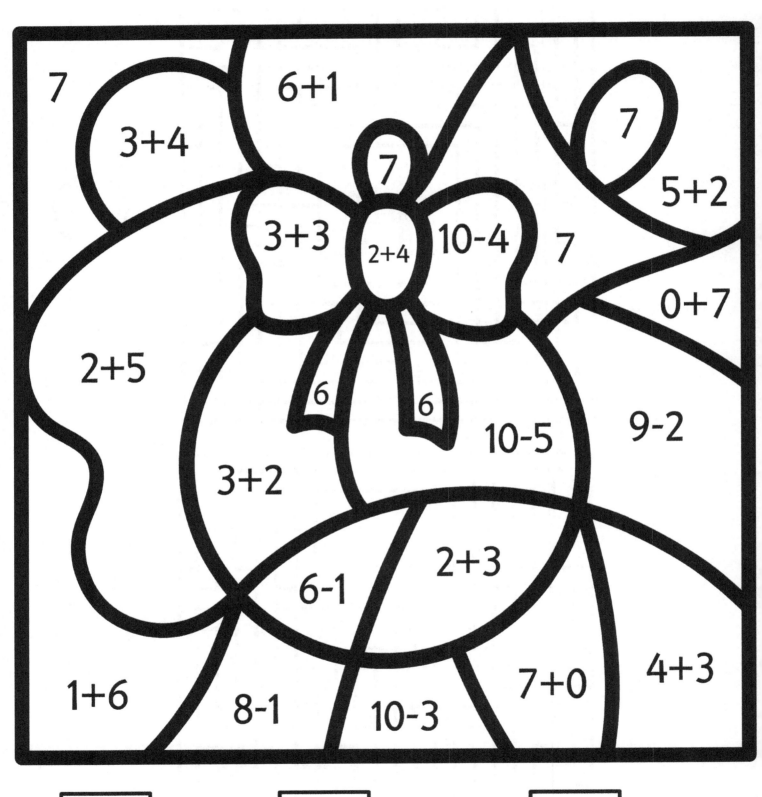

| 5 | red | 6 | yellow | 7 | green |

Christmas Crossword

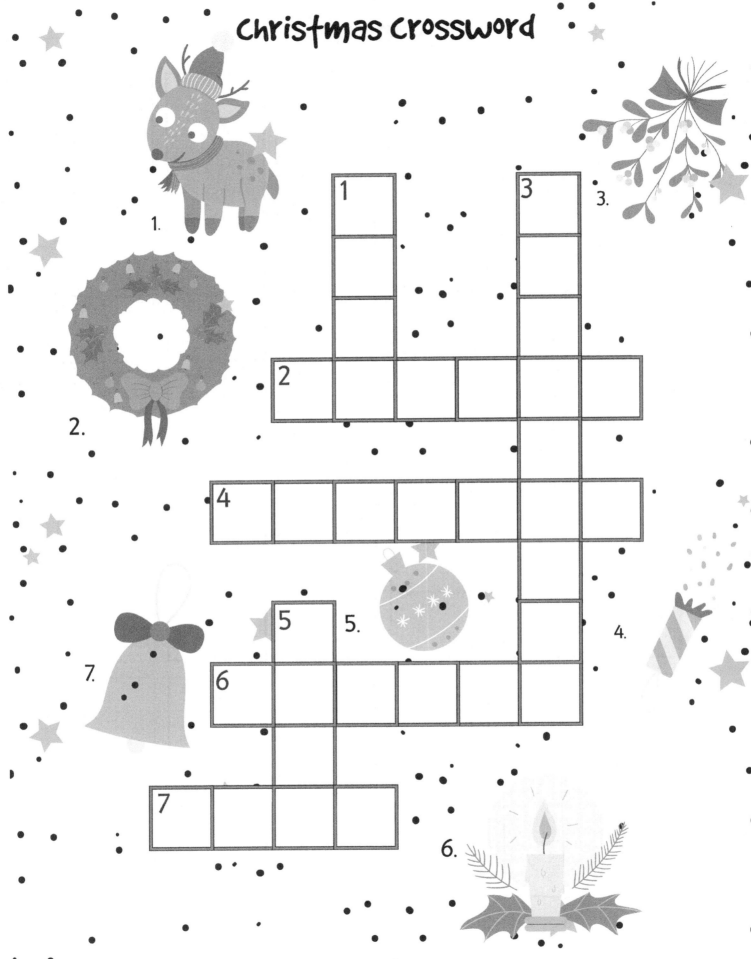

winter word search

Find animals in the picture and in the puzzle

P	E	N	G	U	I	N	B	S	B
F	M	P	O	B	S	R	E	C	U
R	A	C	N	E	M	F	A	H	L
O	F	C	S	U	O	A	R	O	L
L	H	O	O	N	N	L	U	Q	F
L	C	R	S	C	K	E	Y	A	I
A	M	A	U	L	N	F	I	U	N
S	Q	U	I	R	R	E	L	Q	C
O	R	C	O	U	I	H	F	M	H
U	D	E	E	R	L	A	R	E	U

LLAMA   HARE

DEER   RACCOON

BEAR   MONKEY

PENGUIN   SQUIRREL

BULLFINCH

29

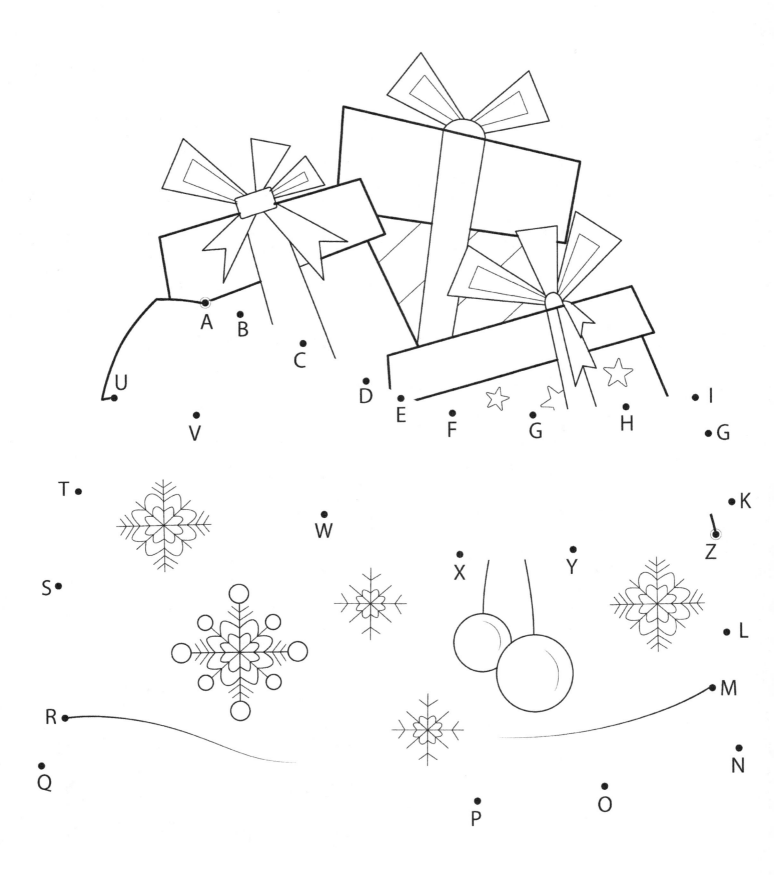

color in

how many ?

PAGE TITLE HERE

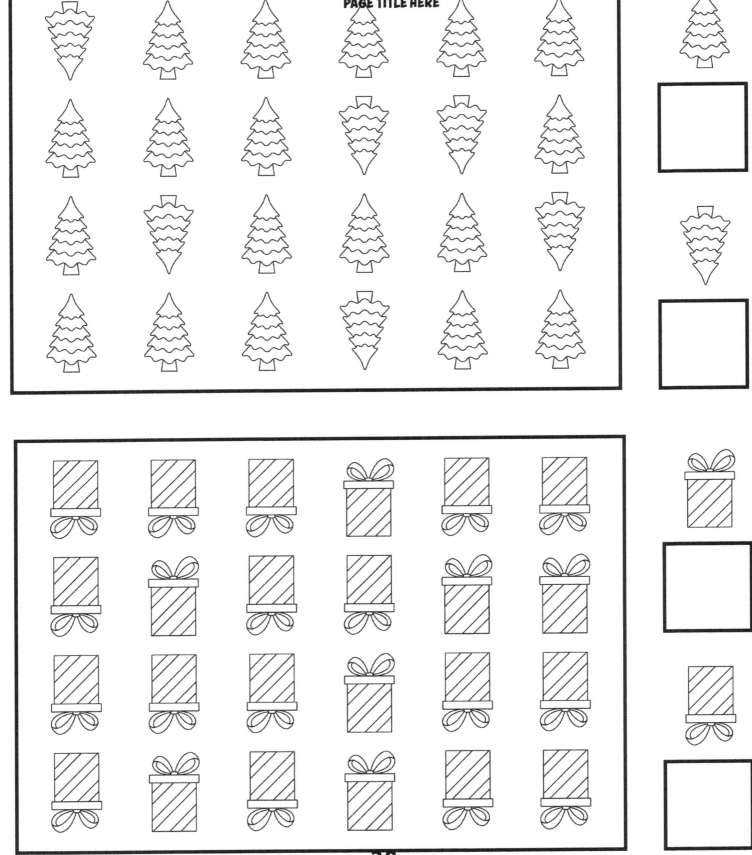

find 10 differences then color in

find 5 differences then color in

33

gingerbread house

color by number

1	2	3	4	5	6	7	8	9
green	red	dark red	brown	yellow	black	orange	blue	beige

35

maze lines - circle the answer

christmas day word search

Y	N	W	Q	U	I	I	N	L	C	M
K	T	R	E	E	S	A	N	T	A	H
V	R	S	S	T	A	R	I	B	F	A
S	G	S	T	O	C	K	I	N	G	T
X	C	A	N	D	Y	B	E	L	L	S
G	I	N	G	E	R	B	R	E	A	D
M	I	N	S	N	O	W	M	A	N	N
S	N	O	W	F	L	A	K	E	V	A
G	B	H	O	L	L	Y	Q	Q	F	F
A	U	W	C	H	I	M	N	E	Y	A

SANTA
CHIMNEY
SNOWFLAKE
HAT
SNOWMAN
GINGERBREAD
STOCKING
CANDY
HOLLY
BELLS
STAR
TREE

how many?

	🛷	❄	❄
	5	0	1
	—	—	—
	—	—	—
	—	—	—
	—	—	—

	🌲	🦊	🦌
	0	0	6
	—	—	—
	—	—	—
	—	—	—
	—	—	—

trace the alphabet

Aa Bb Cc Dd Ee

Ff Gg Hh Ii Jj

Kk Ll Mm Nn

Oo Pp Qq Rr Ss

Tt Uu Vv Ww

Xx Yy Zz

find 10 differences then color in

reindeer and snowman

trace the lines - color in

42

Snowman - copy and color

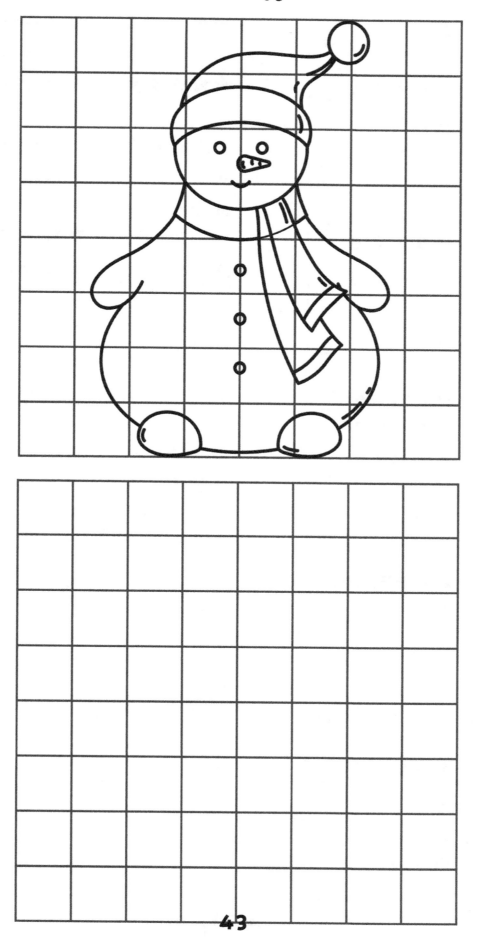

counting game

44

join the dots - trace the lines - color in

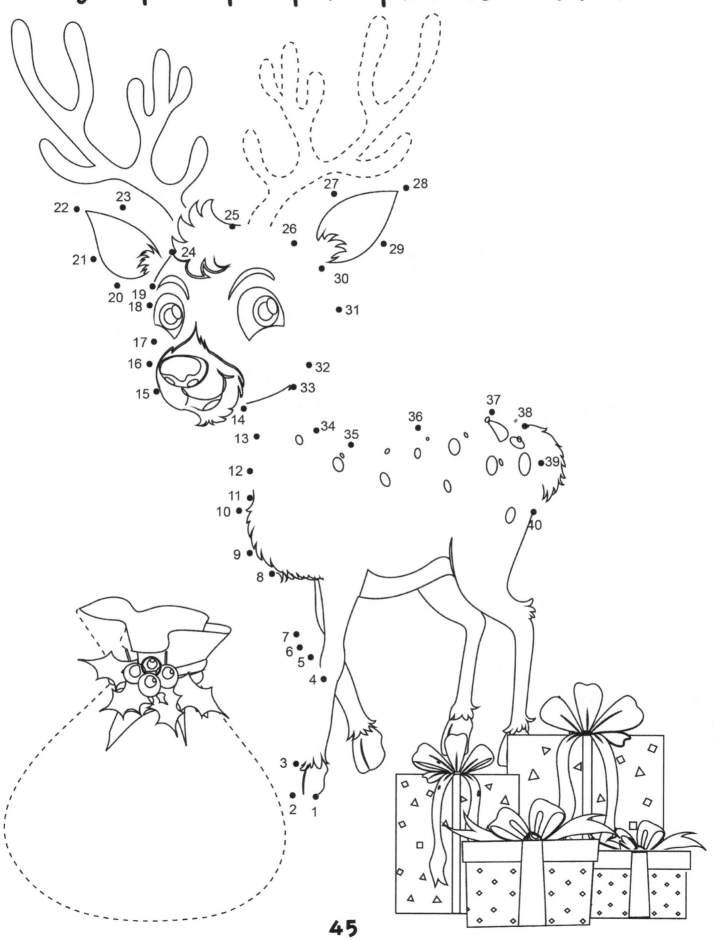

45

christmas crossword

"Christmas day"

Finish

47

trace the words

sock

Santa Claus

Christmas tree

wreath

reindeer

snowman

color by numbers

2	2	2	2	2	2	1	2	2	2	2	2	2
2	1	2	7	7	2	2	2	7	7	2	1	2
2	2	7	2	7	7		7	7	2	7	2	2
2	2	2	7	7	2	5	2	7	7	2	2	2
2	1	2	2	7	5	5	5	7	2	2	1	2
2	2	2	2						2	2	2	2
2	2	4	4	4	4	4	4	4	4	4	2	2
2	4	6	6	4	4	4	4	4	6	6	4	2
2	2	2	2	4	4	4	4	4	2	2	2	2
1	2	2	2	3	4	4	4	3	2	2	2	1
2	2	2	2	4	4	4	4	4	2	2	2	2
2	2	1	2	4	4	6	4	4	2	1	2	2
2	2	2	2	2	4	4	4	2	2	2	2	2
2	1	2	2	2	2	2	2	2	2	2	1	2

1 - blue   2 - light blue   3 - black   4 - brown
5 - red   6 - pink   7 - gray

find 7 differences then color in

maze game

53

how many?

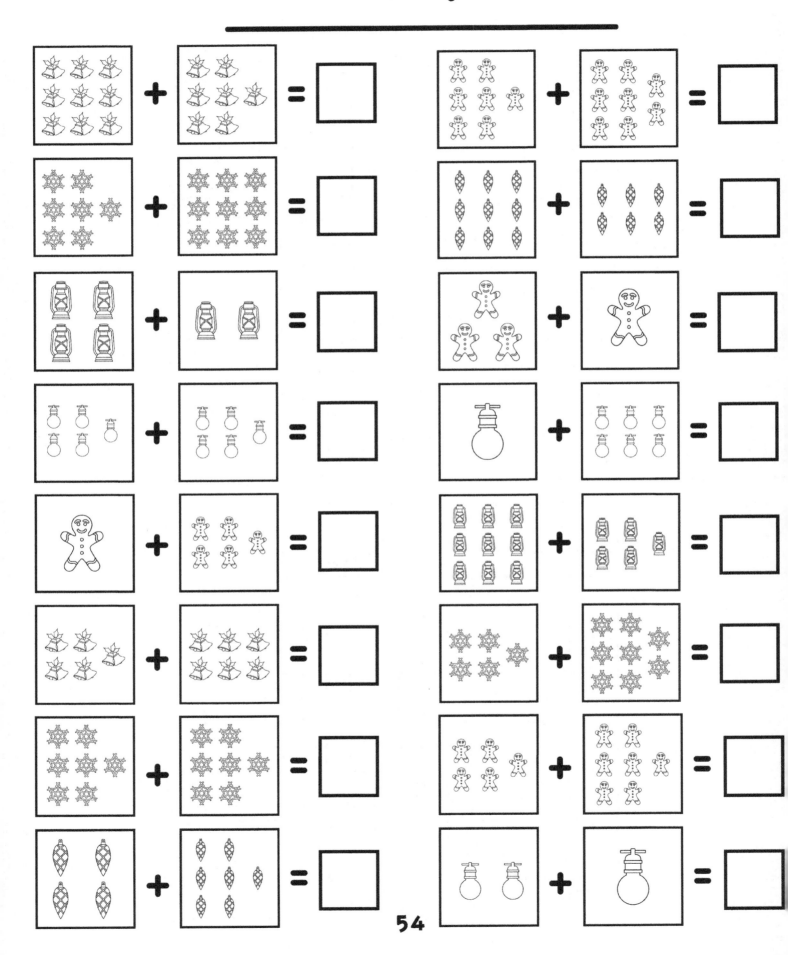

54

number trace 1-10

0   zero   zero

1   one   one

2   two   two

3   three   three

4   four   four

5   five   five

6   six   six

7   seven   seven

8   eight   eight

9   nine   nine

10   ten   ten

count - add - color in

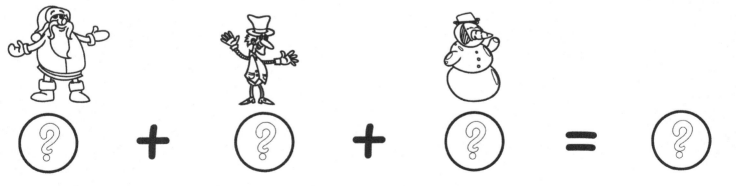

11   eleven

12   twelve

13   thirteen

14   fourteen

15   fifteen

16   sixteen

17   seventeen

18   eighteen

19   nineteen

20   twenty

word search

winter snow present star

elf candle holiday

santa sleigh clock frost

E H O L I D A Y
S T S T A R S P
A S L E I G H R
N E C L O C K E
T F R O S T W S
A W I N T E R E
S N O W E L F N
S C A N D L E T

What is in the box?

59

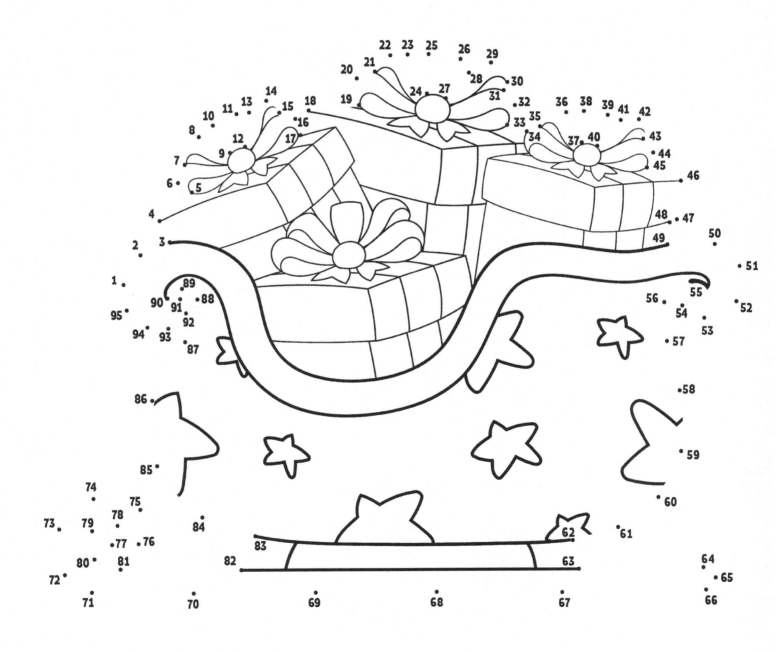

color by number

1	2	3	4	5	6
green	yellow	orange	red	blue	pink

find 10 differences then color in

find 5 differences then color in

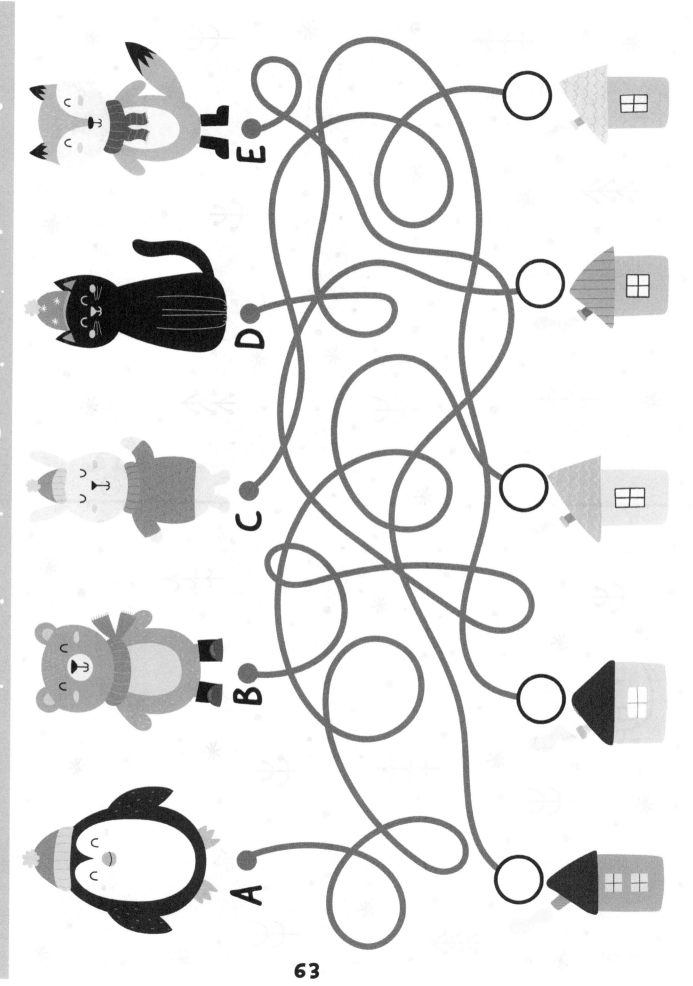

E

D

C

B

A

find the shadow

64

SUDOKU

find 7 differences

santa riding a reindeer

Count to 29 – fill in the blanks

trace the lines - color in

how many?

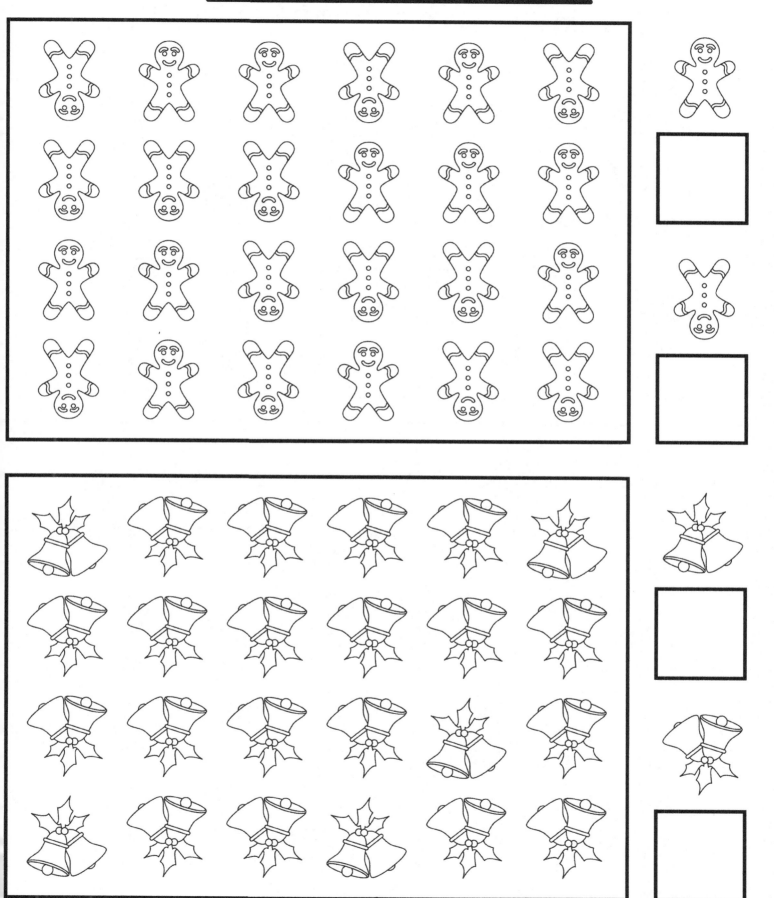

FIND
ONE
OF A KIND
?

FIND
ONE
OF A KIND
?

74

maze game

find the path from 1 to 10

5	8	2	6	7	3	
4	6	7	8	4	2	
8	2	5	4	2	5	1	1
7	10	6	9	6	5	3	2
	10	9	8	7	4	5
	9	7	8	6	5	7

find the path from 1 to 20

1 4 1 7 11 8 6 7 9

1 5 7 8 14 12 13 14 12

11 1 2 3 4 11 12 11 18 15 9

4 2 3 7 5 9 15 10 17 16 13

5 7 4 11 6 7 8 9 18 19 20

7 9 5 6 7 15 20 17 19

9 11 8 11 9 16 17 18 17

CHRISTMAS WORD SEARCH PUZZLE

I	D	S	W	Q	S	A	N	T	A	O
V	U	N	V	A	L	G	L	V	E	D
B	J	O	P	R	E	S	E	N	T	A
E	W	W	Z	E	I	T	M	K	K	N
L	T	M	T	N	G	O	Z	Z	I	C
L	R	A	E	X	H	C	P	W	A	E
V	N	N	K	T	V	K	D	E	O	E
Q	F	N	W	R	E	I	Q	B	G	L
N	U	Q	S	E	K	N	O	X	Q	F
G	D	X	R	E	G	G	A	U	V	X
R	T	W	R	E	A	T	H	D	P	I

77

find 10 differences

penguins fishing

finish the alphabet - color in

A		C	D	
F	G		I	
K		M		O
	Q		S	
U		W		

80

reindeer – Copy and color

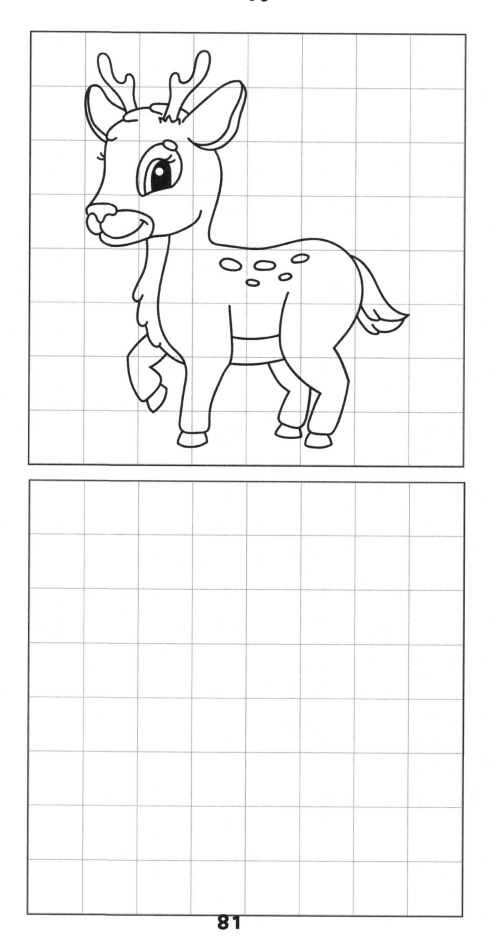

help santa to the fireplace

dot to dot - easy

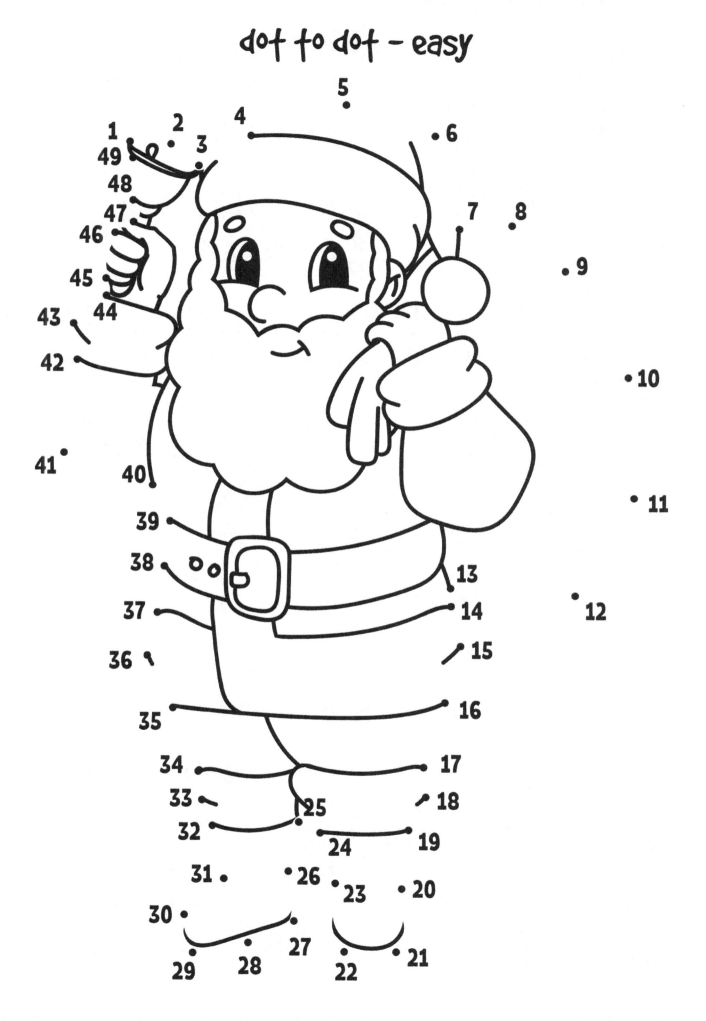

FIND TWO THE SAME PICTURES

FIND TWO THE SAME PICTURES

alphabet maze

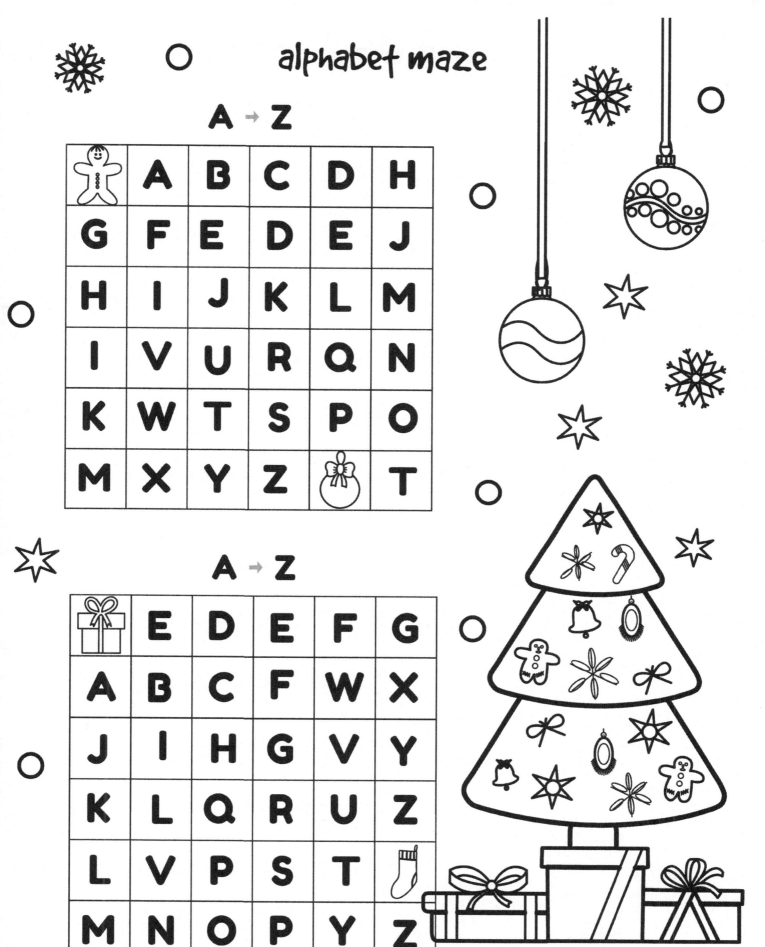

A → Z

	A	B	C	D	H
G	F	E	D	E	J
H	I	J	K	L	M
I	V	U	R	Q	N
K	W	T	S	P	O
M	X	Y	Z		T

A → Z

	E	D	E	F	G
A	B	C	F	W	X
J	I	H	G	V	Y
K	L	Q	R	U	Z
L	V	P	S	T	
M	N	O	P	Y	Z

Christmas Crossword

color by numbers

1 - purple   2 - light blue   3 - yellow   4 - orange

5 - blue   6 - beige   7 - red

how many ?

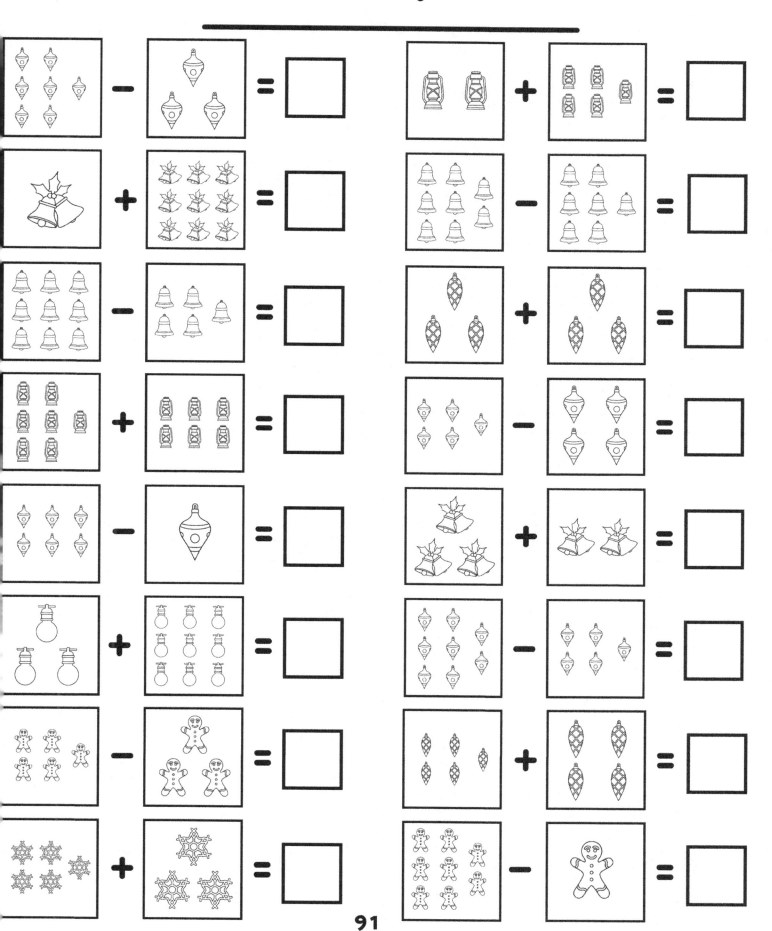

HOW MANY

SANTAS

DO YOU SEE?

how many?

	4	1	1
	—	—	—
	—	—	—
	—	—	—
	—	—	—
	—	—	—

	1	3	2
	—	—	—
	—	—	—
	—	—	—
	—	—	—

93

Christmas Word Search

S	N	O	O	S	N	O	W	M	A	N	U	D	W	A
L	E	I	C	T	B	L	W	I	N	T	C	E	I	G
E	R	T	H	R	R	I	E	W	T	W	H	E	N	I
I	O	W	R	E	A	T	H	P	R	G	R	R	M	N
G	L	E	I	T	P	G	A	R	N	H	R	T	E	G
H	W	Q	S	N	R	T	R	E	E	T	N	I	A	E
S	A	N	T	A	E	N	W	S	D	S	U	N	W	R
M	F	S	M	U	S	S	Z	E	D	E	E	S	A	B
E	K	L	A	M	E	C	E	N	B	G	W	N	E	R
R	L	E	S	E	W	I	N	T	E	R	I	O	L	E
B	E	G	W	S	I	R	D	S	L	I	N	W	L	A
E	S	H	I	N	N	S	E	N	R	N	C	S	Y	D
L	I	O	M	H	O	L	L	Y	L	G	D	A	H	E
L	T	R	E	C	H	M	A	R	L	I	G	H	T	S
S	N	O	W	F	L	A	K	E	S	G	I	N	G	D

SNOWFLAKES   CHRISTMAS   LIGHTS   GINGERBREAD
SNOW   PRESENTS   SANTA   SNOWMAN
BELLS   TREE   WREATH   WINTER
HOLLY   DEER   SLEIGH

94

father christmas maze

95

color by number

1	2	3	4	5	6	7
red	blue	yellow	brown	pink	grey	green

Inside other books for ages 4-8 from SamiraTAJ.com

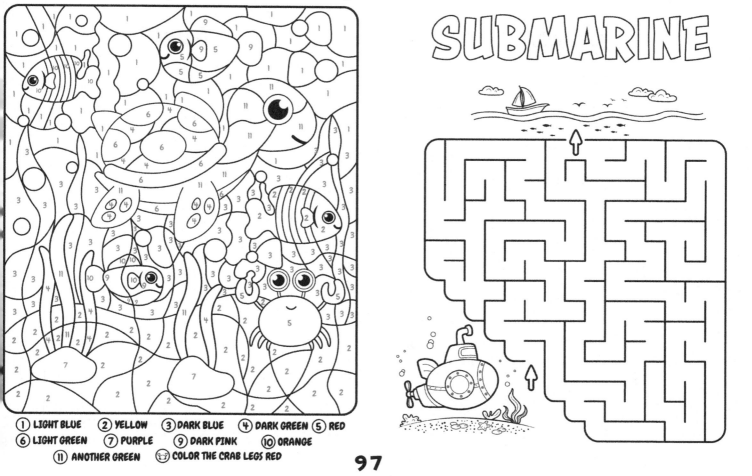

SUBMARINE

① LIGHT BLUE ② YELLOW ③ DARK BLUE ④ DARK GREEN ⑤ RED
⑥ LIGHT GREEN ⑦ PURPLE ⑨ DARK PINK ⑩ ORANGE
⑪ ANOTHER GREEN COLOR THE CRAB LEGS RED

LOVED
A feeling of strong or constant affection.

Inside other books for ages 4-8 from SamiraTAJ.com

SPORTS

B	T	X	E	Z	T	Q	F
A	J	Q	O	T	E	C	O
S	S	O	X	U	N	R	O
E	N	O	I	A	N	G	T
B	B	E	C	K	I	O	B
A	A	T	R	C	S	L	A
L	G	F	L	N	E	F	L
L	P	E	S	D	P	R	L

BASEBALL FOOTBALL
GOLF SOCCER
TENNIS

SPORTS

Across
[3] American summertime sport.

Down
[1] The sport played at the Super Bowl.

[2] The sport played with a stick and little white ball.

[4] Sport played with hitting a ball over a net.

98

solutions & suggestions

Please consider leaving an honest review
to let us know how your Little Genius
found our Puzzle book.

This helps other buyers make informed decisions.

samirataj.com

christmas crossword 4

"Christmas day"

FIND TWO
THE SAME
PICTURES

FIND TWO
THE SAME
PICTURES

6

finish the alphabet - color in 8

A	B	C	D	E
F	G	H	I	J
K	L	M	N	O
P	Q	R	S	T
U	V	W	X	Y
Z				

how many ? 9

5	6	2	7	3	2
2	5	10	4	6	1
3	6	10	2	8	10

find 7 differences then color in 12

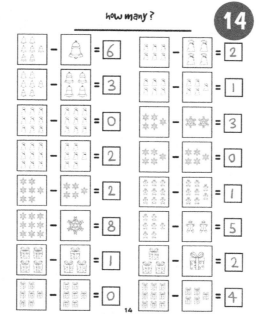

how many ? 14

- = 6   - = 2
- = 3   - = 1
- = 0   - = 3
- = 2   - = 0
- = 2   - = 1
- = 8   - = 5
- = 1   - = 2
- = 0   - = 4

christmas word search 18

STOCKING
SANTA
SNOWMAN
SNOWGLOBE
DEER
PRESENT

S	N	O	W	M	A	N
C	S	T	O	P	R	S
S	N	O	C	H	E	A
D	E	W	K	R	S	N
S	E	G	I	I	E	T
T	R	L	N	G	N	A
M	A	O	B	E	T	S

MATCH THE SAME QUANTITY — 20

4
9
2
1

4
6
7
2

9
1
6
5

3
5
8
1

2
6

5
8

find 10 differences then color in — 23

fill in the blanks - help thr reindeer reach sa — 24

39 38 37 36 35
40 30 34
29 31 33
25 28 32
24 26 27
23 18 17 16
22 21 20 19 15
14
9 10 11 12 13
8
7
6 5 4 3 2 1

who gets to the present? — 25

1 2 3

2

3

1 3

how many? — 27

7 | 1 | 6 | 5 | 3 | 8

8 | 5 | 2 | 9 | 9 | 10

8 | 3 | 9 | 4 | 8 | 1

christmas crossword — 28

1. D E E R
3. M I S T L E T O
2. W R E A T H
4. C R A C K E R
5. B
6. C A N D L E
   B L
7. B E L L

winter word search — 29

Find animals in the picture and in the puzzle

P E N G U I N B S B
F M P O B S R E C U
R A C N E M F A H L
O F C S U O A R O L
L H O O N N L U Q F
L C R S C K E Y A I
A M A U L N F I U N
S Q U I R R E L Q C
O R C O U I H F M H
U D E E R L A R E U

LLAMA   HARE
DEER   RACCOON
BEAR   MONKEY
PENGUIN   SQUIRREL
BULLFINCH

how many? — 32

PAGE TITLE HERE

18

6

7

17

find 10 differences then color in — 33

find 5 differences then color in

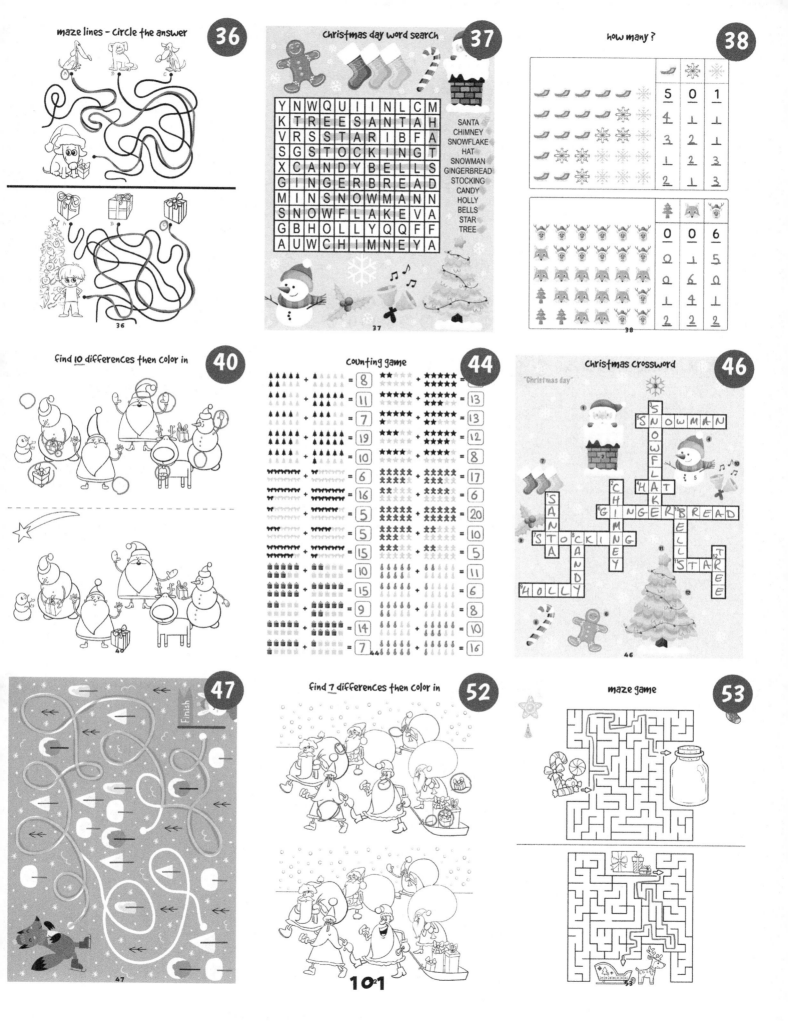

36 — maze lines - circle the answer

37 — christmas day word search

```
Y N W Q U I I N L C M
K T R E E S A N T A H
V R S S T A R I B F A
S G S T O C K I N G T
X C A N D Y B E L L S
G I N G E R B R E A D
M I N S N O W M A N N
S N O W F L A K E V A
G B H O L L Y Q Q F F
A U W C H I M N E Y A
```

SANTA
CHIMNEY
SNOWFLAKE
HAT
SNOWMAN
GINGERBREAD
STOCKING
CANDY
HOLLY
BELLS
STAR
TREE

38 — how many ?

	🧦	❄	❄
	5	0	1
	4	1	1
	3	2	1
	1	2	3
	2	1	3

	🌲	🦊	🦌
	0	0	6
	0	1	5
	0	6	0
	1	4	1
	2	2	2

40 — find 10 differences then color in

44 — counting game

🌲+🌲 = 8   ⭐⭐+⭐⭐⭐⭐⭐ =
🌲+🌲 = 11   ⭐⭐⭐⭐⭐+⭐⭐⭐ = 13
🌲+🌲 = 7   ⭐⭐⭐⭐⭐+⭐⭐⭐⭐⭐ = 13
🌲+🌲 = 19   ⭐⭐⭐+⭐⭐⭐⭐⭐ = 12
🌲+🌲 = 10   ⭐⭐⭐+⭐⭐⭐⭐ = 8
🎀+🎀 = 6   ⭐⭐⭐⭐+⭐⭐⭐ = 17
🎀+🎀 = 16   ⭐⭐+⭐⭐⭐⭐ = 6
🎀+🎀 = 5   ⭐⭐⭐⭐⭐+⭐⭐⭐⭐⭐ = 20
🎀+🎀 = 5   ⭐⭐⭐⭐⭐+⭐⭐ = 10
🎀+🎀 = 15   ⭐⭐⭐+⭐⭐ = 5
🎁+🎁 = 10   + = 11
🎁+🎁 = 15   + = 6
🎁+🎁 = 9   + = 8
🎁+🎁 = 14   + = 10
🎁+🎁 = 7   + = 16

46 — christmas crossword

"Christmas day"

SNOWMAN
SNOWFLAKE
HAT
SANTA
GINGERBREAD
CHIMNEY
CANDY
STOCKING
BELL
STAR
TREE
HOLLY

47

Finish

52 — find 7 differences then color in

101

53 — maze game

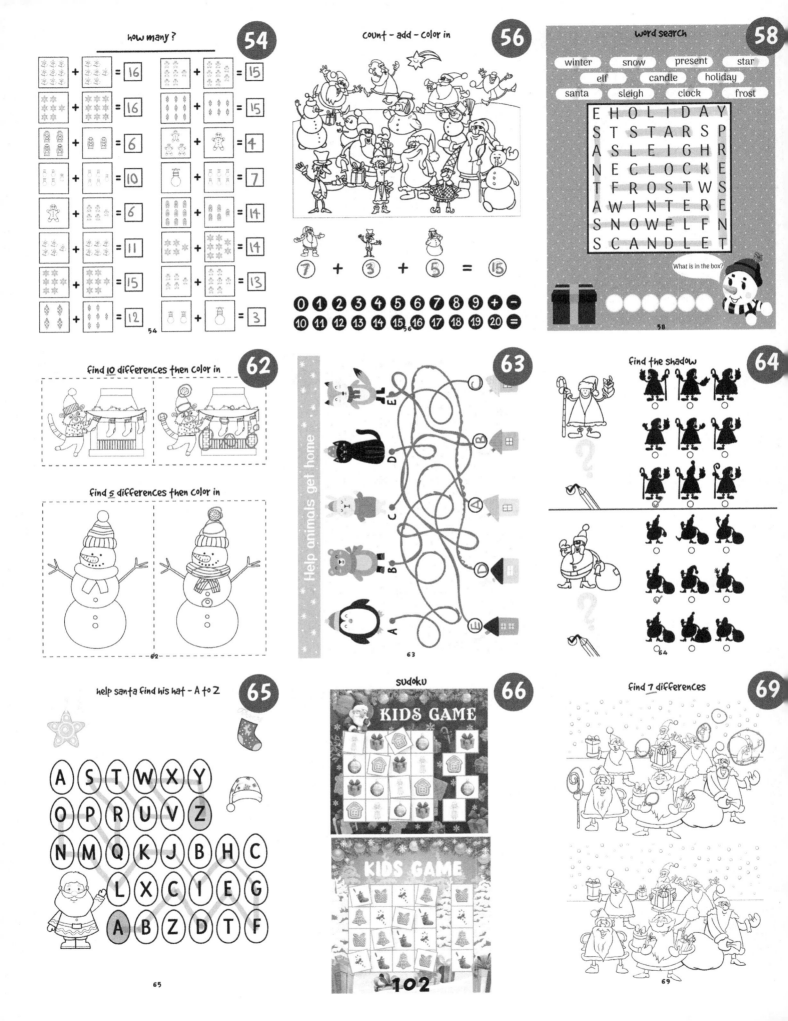

54 — how many?

☃ + ☃ = 16		❄ + ❄ = 15
❄ + ❄ = 16		✦ + ✦ = 15
🎁 + 🎁 = 6		🍪 + 🍪 = 4
🔔 + 🔔 = 10		⛄ + ⛄ = 7
🍪 + 🍪 = 6		🔔 + 🔔 = 14
❄ + ❄ = 11		❄ + ❄ = 14
❄ + ❄ = 15		✦ + ✦ = 13
✦ + ✦ = 12		⛄ + ⛄ = 3

56 — count – add – color in

7 + 3 + 5 = 15

0 1 2 3 4 5 6 7 8 9 + −
10 11 12 13 14 15 16 17 18 19 20 =

58 — word search

winter   snow   present   star
elf   candle   holiday
santa   sleigh   clock   frost

```
E H O L I D A Y
S T S T A R S P
A S L E I G H R
N E C L O C K E
T F R O S T W S
A W I N T E R E
S N O W E L F N
S C A N D L E T
```

What is in the box?

62 — find 10 differences then color in

find 5 differences then color in

63 — Help animals get home

64 — find the shadow

65 — help santa find his hat – A to Z

A	S	T	W	X	Y
O	P	R	U	V	Z
N	M	Q	K	J	B	H	C
L	X	C	I	E	G
A	B	Z	D	T	F

66 — sudoku

KIDS GAME

KIDS GAME

69 — find 7 differences

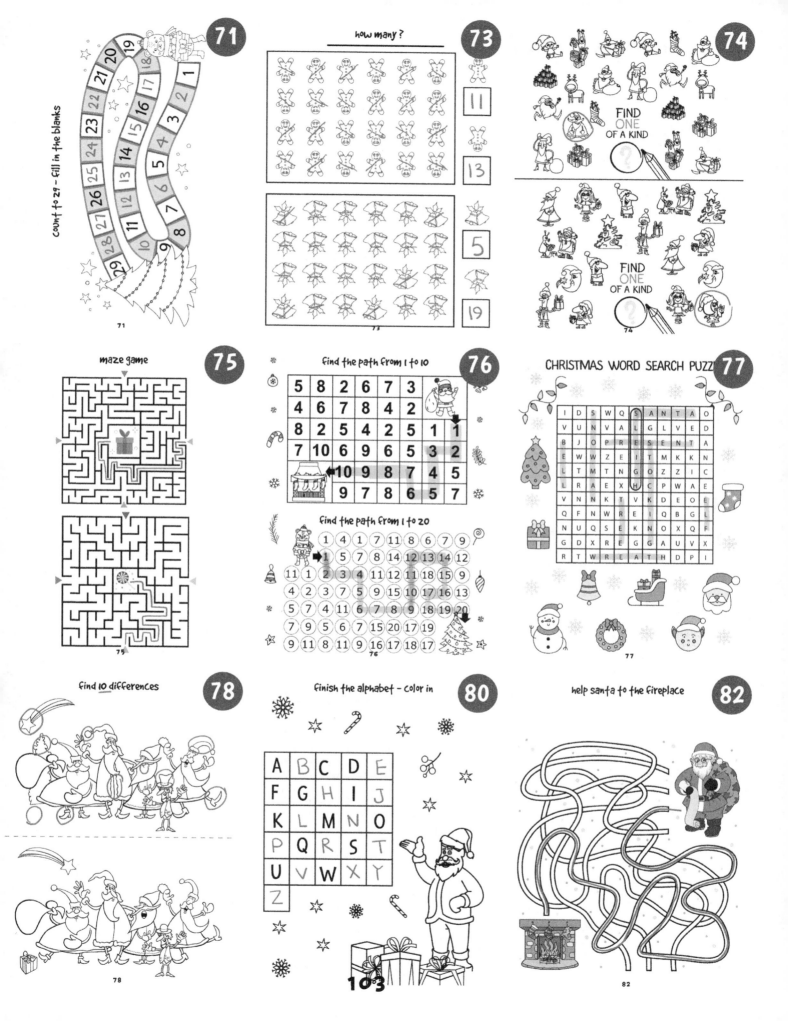

71
count to 29 – fill in the blanks

19 18
20 17 1
21 16 2
22 15 3
23 14 4
24 13 5
25 12 6
26 11 7
27 11 8
28 10 9
29 9 8

73
how many ?

11

13

5

19

74
FIND ONE OF A KIND

FIND ONE OF A KIND

75
maze game

76
find the path from 1 to 10

5	8	2	6	7	3
4	6	7	8	4	2
8	2	5	4	2	5	1	1
7	10	6	9	6	5	3	2
10	9	8	7	4	5
9	7	8	6	5	7

find the path from 1 to 20

77
CHRISTMAS WORD SEARCH PUZZLE

I	D	S	W	Q	S	A	N	T	A	O
V	U	N	V	A	L	G	L	V	E	D
B	J	O	P	R	E	S	E	N	T	A
E	W	W	Z	E	I	T	M	K	K	N
L	T	M	T	N	G	O	Z	Z	I	C
L	R	A	E	X	H	C	P	W	A	E
V	N	N	K	T	V	K	D	E	O	E
Q	F	N	W	R	E	I	Q	B	G	L
N	U	Q	S	E	K	N	O	X	Q	F
G	D	X	R	E	G	G	A	U	V	X
R	T	W	R	E	A	T	H	D	P	I

78
find 10 differences

80
finish the alphabet – color in

A	B	C	D	E
F	G	H	I	J
K	L	M	N	O
P	Q	R	S	T
U	V	W	X	Y
Z

82
help santa to the fireplace

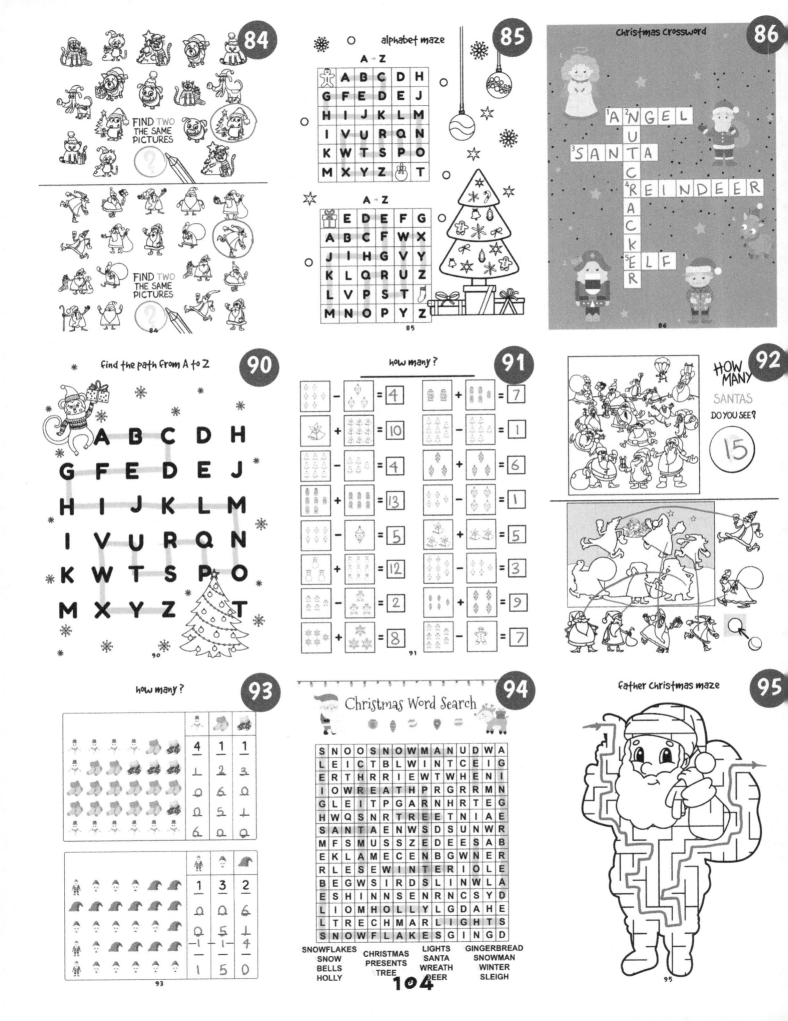

Christmas
ACTIVITY BOOK

DOWNLOAD YOUR
COLOR CERTIFICATE
AT SamiraTAJ.COM

CERTIFICATE
OF COMPLETION

AWARDED TO : _____

AGE : _____   DATE : _____

MORE BOOKS

SamiraTAJ has many full color vibrantly illustrated activity books, well thought out puzzle books, and coloring books for your Little Genius.

Designed to help little ones practice and improve their fine motor skills, auditory attention, and concentration. Working through the books together will boost your child's academic confidence.

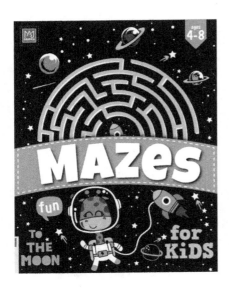
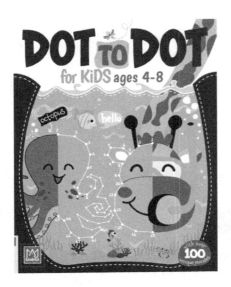
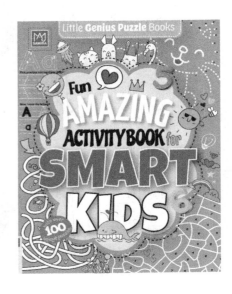
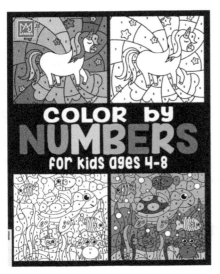

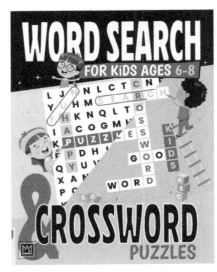

samirataj.com

Made in the USA
Coppell, TX
03 December 2022